Where will you go, Ricky Jo?

Written by Tom Murdoch

Illustrated by Marina Veselinovic

Last night I was sleeping,
   When my dream said to me,
"Ricky Jo, Ricky Jo,
   there are places to see."

You're off on adventure far and wide?
Try new things you've never tried?
Are you sure you'll be careful wherever you go?
Will you tell us your stories, Ricky Jo?

Where will you go, Ricky Jo?

Down to the store to buy new shoes
     With socks in bright colors of reds and blues
a shirt in bright yellow, green and pink
     Look in the mirror. What do you think?

That's where you'll go, Ricky Jo.

Where will you go, Ricky Jo?

Would you walk through the gardens of flowers and trees?
Watch all the butterflies and hear all the bees.
The blossoms smell nice,
but they all make you sneeze!

That's where you'll go, Ricky Jo.

Where will you go, Ricky Jo?

Across the oceans,
Deep and blue
With whales and sails
And turtles too.

That's where you'll go, Ricky Jo.

Where will you go, Ricky Jo?

Would you climb the tall mountains
All covered in snow,
Button your coat
before you go.

That's where you'll go, Ricky Jo.

Where will you go, Ricky Jo?

Ride in the fire truck
  all shiny and red.
Turn on the siren,
  put a hat on your head!

That's where you'll go, Ricky Jo.

Where will you go, Ricky Jo?

Fly in an airplane
    Way up in the sky
Above all the clouds,
    Now that's very high!

That's where you'll go, Ricky Jo.

Where will you go, Ricky Jo?

Would you ride a brown horse
across the land
through the tall grass
and over the sand?

That's where you'll go, Ricky Jo.

Where will you go, Ricky Jo?

Will you visit the barnyard,
where animals stay?
Two cows and three chickens
and sheep in the hay!
There's always more chores,
and no time for play.

That's where you'll go, Ricky Jo.

Now the daytime is leaving,
    Night time is here.
Sweet dreams are waiting,
    When sleepy is near.

That's where you'll go, Ricky Jo.

GOOD NIGHT
RICKY JO